1996

MR. MEN AND LITTLE MISS ANNUAL

by Roger Hargreaves

New Illustrations by Adam Hargreaves
Compiled by Brenda Apsley
Editor: Nina Filipek   Designer: Paul Dronsfield

© Mrs Roger Hargreaves 1995.
Printed and published 1995 under licence from
Price Stern Sloan Inc., Los Angeles.
All rights reserved.
Published in Great Britain by World International,
an imprint of Egmont Publishing Ltd,
Egmont House, PO Box 111, Great Ducie Street,
Manchester M60 3BL.
Printed in Great Britain
ISBN 07498 2406 9

CONTENTS

Hello, I'm little Miss Sunshine! For the first time ever you can find ALL my MR. MEN and LITTLE MISS friends in one book.

There are stories, puzzles, quizzes, recipes and funny poems, too. Oh, and I nearly forgot - there is a fantastic MR. MEN competition to enter. Must go now - I'm running in a race on page 46. Look out for me.

Bye! Have fun!

Find me on every page!

MR. TICKLE'S SPECIAL DAY

1. Mr Tickle is a very jolly-looking Mr Man. He is small and round and has arms that stretch and stretch. Extraordinarily long arms!

2. But Mr Tickle was unhappy. No one ever walked past his house because they knew that if they did, he would tickle them.

3. One morning he was surprised to see Mr Happy come walking by. "This is my lucky day!" smiled Mr Tickle. "What fun!"

4. Mr Tickle reached out of his window and tickled Mr Happy. Mr Happy giggled, then smiled happily. So did Mr Tickle.

5. Mr Funny came along, so Mr Tickle tickled him, too. He even managed to tickle Mr Bounce as he bounced by. Mr Tickle could not believe his luck.

6. Along came Mr Bump and Mr Greedy, so he tickled them, too, one with each long arm.

A VERY HAPPY BIRTHDAY TO MR TICKLE

He's here! He's there! Beware! Beware! Mr Tickle is everywhere!

7. More and more Mr Men came that day. Can you guess why? They had all come to be tickled as a special treat for Mr Tickle's birthday! It was the very best present he had ever had!

MR. NOSEY AND THE BEES

Mr Nosey poked his nose
Into a hive of bees!
So off to Mr Bump he went,
And said, "Oh please, oh please!
Can I have a bandage,
To stop me feeling ill?"
Mr Bump gave him a bandage,

And then gave him the bill!

LITTLE MISS HELPFUL'S PARTY SANDWICHES

Little Miss Helpful likes being helpful. She helped Miss Giggles by making some special sandwiches for her birthday party. Why not try making some? Miss Helpful will show you how. Remember, always ask a grown-up to help you in the kitchen.

YOU WILL NEED:
2 slices of brown bread
2 slices of white bread
butter or margarine
50g cream cheese
2 teaspoons tomato ketchup
50g peanut butter
2 teaspoons strawberry jam

Mmm!
They taste good!
Giggle, giggle!

1. Ask a grown-up to cut the crusts off the slices of bread.
2. Spread butter or margarine on each slice.
3. Spread the cream cheese on the slices of brown bread. Add the tomato ketchup.
4. Spread the peanut butter on the white bread. Add the strawberry jam.
5. Roll up each slice of bread into a sausage shape. Roll the bread tightly.
6. Cut the rolls into slices about 1cm wide, to make little circle shaped sandwiches.

10

LOTS OF EGGS FOR MR. STRONG

Mr Strong is the strongest person in the world. The secret of his great strength is – eggs! The more eggs Mr Strong eats, the stronger he becomes. When Mr Strong helped a farmer one day, the farmer told him he could take home as many eggs as he liked.

Count how many eggs Mr Strong is carrying home!
How many brown eggs? How many white eggs?
How many speckled eggs? How many eggs altogether?

BROWN   WHITE   SPECKLED

Answers:
6 brown eggs, 9 white eggs and
8 speckled eggs; 23 altogether.

11

MR. SNEEZE'S

1. Mr Sneeze sneezes louder than anyone else. "ATISHOO!"

2. He got a job in a park, sweeping up all the leaves.

3. He collected all the leaves and put them into a big bin.

4. The park was nice and tidy now. But more leaves fell from the trees. And more. "I'll never finish this job!" he sighed.

5. Mr Sneeze sneezed a big sneeze. A really big sneeze. "ATISHOO!"

6. His sneeze blew the leaves out of the bin. It blew the leaves off the trees. There was not a leaf left in the park. Well done, Mr Sneeze!

All About MR. LAZY

home: Yawn Cottage, Sleepyland
colour: pink
hat: blue
favourite place: bed
likes: sleeping
dislikes: Mr Busy

Mr Lazy cannot sleep,
So Mr Lazy's counting sheep.
Ninety-three and
Ninety-four!
Ninety-five and
Ninety...
SNORE!

13

MR. HAPPY'S
SMILE PUZZLE

Mr Happy lives in Happyland. He is fat, and round, and happy! He always has a big smile on his face. But he isn't the only Mr Man who has a smile on his face.

Can you match the smiles on this page to the right Mr Men? Why not draw them on their faces to make them look happy?

Mr Happy

Mr Busy

Mr Greedy

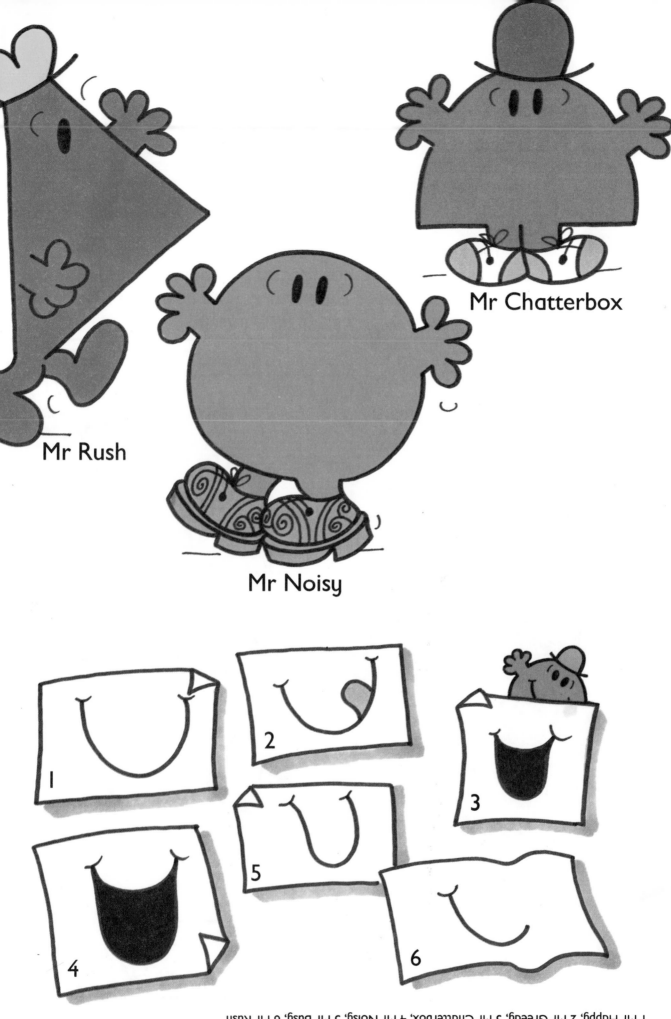

Mr Rush

Mr Chatterbox

Mr Noisy

1

2

3

5

4

6

MR. FORGETFUL'S PROBLEM

Mr Forgetful has a problem. He has nearly finished his jigsaw puzzle, but he has forgotten which of the pieces he has left will complete the picture. Can you help him? Which piece, 1, 2, 3, 4 or 5, will fit?

Answer:
Piece 4 will fit.

16

LITTLE MISS CONTRARY

"Mary, Mary, Miss Contrary,
How does your garden grow?"

"With silver bells and cockle shells,
And pretty maids all in a row!"

How many cockle shells can you count in Miss Contrary's garden?

Answer:
12 cockle shells

17

MR. NOISY
AND THE WORMS

Mr Noisy is a very noisy person. "My grass needs cutting!" he shouted one morning. He got out his lawnmower and walked across the garden in his big shoes. Clump, clump, clump! he went.

"Tra-la-la," he sang. What a lot of noise he made!

In the soil underneath the grass the worms were trying to rest. But it was too noisy for them. They popped their heads out of the ground.

"Do you have to be so noisy?" one worm grumbled.

"You've given me a headache!" said another.

Mr Noisy was sorry. He stopped singing and tiptoed across the grass. But rumble, rumble, rumble! went the mower.

The worms still couldn't sleep. "More noise," they sighed.

"Really, Mr Noisy," said the worms. "Can't you keep that mower quiet?"

"But I must cut the grass," said Mr Noisy.

Then one of the worms had an idea. He wriggled away and came back with some rabbit friends. Lots of them. The rabbits nibbled the grass, and they did it quietly.

Mr Noisy was pleased.

So were the worms.

LITTLE MISS MAGIC'S
MAGIC TRICK

I'm going to show you how to stick a pin into a balloon WITHOUT BURSTING IT!

Blow up two round balloons. Don't blow them up too much.

They should be slightly soft.

Tie a knot in the ends.

Stick a piece of clear sticky tape on to ONE balloon. Smooth it out.

Ask one of your audience to stick a large needle into the balloon without the sticky tape. It will burst, BANG! Now push the pin into the other balloon, but make sure you push it through the patch of sticky tape. The balloon won't burst. Magic!

19

All About MR. QUIET

size:	small
colour:	yellowy-green
nose:	yellowy-green
hair:	five black ones
birthplace:	a cottage in the middle of a wood in Loudland
likes:	quiet
dislikes:	noise
favourite word:	Sssssh!
best friend:	Mr Happy
new home:	Happyland
job:	works in the Happy Lending Library

HAPPY LENDING LIBRARY

LITTLE MISS GREEDY
AND THE SAUSAGES

Little Miss Greedy will eat almost anything, but what she likes best is juicy fat sausages. One day the butcher asked Miss Greedy to help him. "Will you count all the sausages for me, please?" he asked. "I need 20, and you can have the rest to take home." Miss Greedy was in little Miss heaven!

There were sausages everywhere! Can you help Miss Greedy to count them all? How many will she be able to take home to eat after she has given the butcher 20?

21

Answer:
There are 28 sausages. The butcher needs 20, so Miss Greedy can take 8 home to eat.

MR. FUNNY'S FUNNY DAY

1. Mr Funny loves doing funny things to make the other Mr Men laugh and feel happy. He likes pulling funny faces best of all.

2. But today Mr Funny just didn't feel funny. In fact he felt very sad. He couldn't manage a smile – not even a small one.

3. He met Mr Grumble and pulled a funny face to try and make him laugh. But Mr Grumble just said, "Bah! Out of my way!"

4. Mr Funny met Mr Grumpy. He pulled his funniest face. But Mr Grumpy frowned. "This just isn't my funny day," Mr Funny said.

5. Mr Funny walked along feeling very sad. He didn't notice an icy puddle. He slipped on the ice and up he went, right into the air.

6. Mr Funny held on to the branch of a tree. This wasn't funny at all. "Oh dear, how am I going to get down?" he wondered.

7. Mr Funny was still wondering what to do when – CRACK! – the branch snapped, and Mr Funny dropped out of the tree, head first.

8. He landed with a THUD and a CRUMP on his tall yellow hat. The hat was very squashed, but Mr Funny wasn't hurt at all.

9. The Mr Men smiled when they saw Mr Funny. Even Mr Grumble and Mr Grumpy. "They're happy and so am I!" smiled Mr Funny.

23

LITTLE MISS CHATTERBOX'S
SPOT THE DIFFERENCES PUZZLE

Hello, I'm Miss Chatterbox, and I just can't stop chattering. I can talk all day long about all sorts of things. I have a brother called Mr Chatterbox who lives in a box-shaped cottage. Can you guess what it is called? Yes, that's right, Chatterbox Cottage. We are very alike, you know. We are both pink and we both wear blue and white shoes, but I have yellow hair and my brother wears a green hat, and did I tell you that.....

If Miss Chatterbox goes on chattering much longer, there will be no space left for her puzzle! Look at these two pictures of her with her brother, Mr Chatterbox.

Can you find 5 things that are different in the picture on the right?

Answers:
1. Miss Chatterbox is wearing ribbons in her hair,
2. One of Miss Chatterbox's shoes is missing, 3. Mr Chatterbox has his mouth closed (for once!), 4. Mr Chatterbox is wearing a different hat, 5. Miss Chatterbox has a big red nose!

MR. BOUNCE
at Wimbledon

Mr Bounce went to Wimbledon,
But what he didn't deserve,
Was that, while he was there
He was thrown in the air...
And ended up as a serve!

BOUNCE!

All About MR. BOUNCE

size: small
likes: bouncing around
like a tennis ball

colour: yellow
hat: pink
friend: Dr Makeyouwell
likes: buses
dislikes: tennis!

LITTLE MISS SHY
AND
LITTLE MISS TWINS

Little Miss Shy had to find the little
Miss Twins to give them an important
message, when Miss Bossy saw her.
"WHO ARE YOU LOOKING FOR?"
she asked in her loud, bossy voice.
Miss Shy blushed like a beetroot and
rushed off to hide!

Can you find little Miss Twins
and Miss Shy?

LITTLE MISS LUCKY

This is a story about little Miss Lucky. Some words are missing. Look at the little picture clues to find out what they are.

Little Miss Lucky lives on top of a [hill] in a house called [Horseshoe] Cottage.

One night she went to [bed] with a [book]. She loved to read in bed. It was a cold night, so she snuggled down under a thick [blanket]. Miss Lucky heard a knock at the front [door] and went to see who it was. There was nobody there!

She went outside. Nobody!

Suddenly a big gust of wind blew the door shut behind her. BANG! Then it blew her up into the air. Up and up she went, higher than the [cloud].

I wonder why this story is called little Miss Lucky?

Suddenly the wind stopped blowing and Miss Lucky fell to the ground. She landed in a [bush], so she wasn't hurt. In the dark, Miss Lucky bumped into a [tree]. It had a face! And it started to chase her! Miss Lucky ran away as fast as her [feet] could carry her. The tree ran, too, THUD, THUD, THUD! Miss Lucky stopped and shut her [eyes] tight. She was very frightened.

I wonder why her name is Miss Lucky?

THUD! Miss Lucky opened her eyes. The book had fallen off the bed. She had been asleep. It had all been a dream!

So now you know why this story is called little Miss Lucky!

MR. CLEVER and Fred the Flea

Mr Clever had a performing flea,
He trained it to stand on its head.
He even taught it how to speak
And decided to call it...Fred!

All About MR. CLEVER

colour:	orange
hat:	green
title:	The Cleverest Person in the World
favourite saying:	"Oh, I am so very very CLEVER!"
home:	Cleverland
favourite thing:	his special alarm clock, which wakes him up by ringing a bell, switches on a light, says, "Good morning," makes a cup of tea, shows him what the weather is like, tells him the time, and shows him the date, whistling cheerfully while it is doing all that!
dislikes:	jokes

28

LITTLE MISS SPLENDID'S
COLOURS PAGE

"I know everything there is to know about colours, you know. Everything. Can you answer my colours questions?"

1. Which parts of my splendid outfit are RED?

2. What colour is little Miss Sunshine?

3. What colour is little Miss Giggles?

4. Which GREEN little Miss can you see on this page?

5. Which little Miss is PURPLE?

Look at all the other things on the page. Point to them and say what colour they are.

29

Answers:
1. Hat, handbag and shoes, 2. Yellow, 3. Blue, 4. Miss Neat, 5. Miss Naughty.

LITTLE MISS STAR'S
STAR PIZZAS

Little Miss Star lives in Twinkle Cottage. She really wants to be famous, and has tried lots of ways of becoming a star. Her latest idea is to become a famous TV cook. A real star cook. Here is her special recipe for star pizzas. Why not make one?

"Are you famous enough to eat my star pizza? Remember, always ask a grown-up to help you in the kitchen."

FOR EACH STAR PIZZA YOU WILL NEED:

a crumpet
1 teaspoon tomato ketchup
50g hard cheese
1 slice tomato

1. Ask a grown-up to turn on the grill.
2. Grate the cheese. Careful!
3. Use a star-shaped cutter to cut the crumpet into a star shape. If you don't have a cutter, ask a grown-up to cut the crumpet into a star, using a sharp knife.
4. Spread tomato ketchup on top of the crumpet.
5. Put the tomato slice on top.
6. Cover the pizza with grated cheese. You can eat any bits that are left over!
7. Put the pizza under the grill for about 3 or 4 minutes until the cheese has melted. Leave the pizza to cool a little before you eat it.

MR. SILLY'S SILLY DAY

Mr Silly lives in Nonsenseland, where everything is as silly as can be – including Mr Silly!

Mr Silly lives in the silliest-looking house you have ever seen.

One morning Mr Silly was eating his breakfast. "I'm going to wallpaper the house today," he said. He ate a cornflake sandwich, and finished off with a boiled egg – and the shell!

On his way to the shop Mr Silly met a chicken who was wearing wellington boots and carrying an umbrella. "Good morning," said Mr Silly.

"Meow!" said the chicken. Silly chicken!

The wallpaper shop was a silly sort of a shop. Mr Silly liked all the wallpapers. He couldn't decide which he liked best, so he bought one roll of each pattern!

As Mr Silly came out of the wallpaper shop carrying his wallpaper and paste, it started to rain. He went to the baker's shop – which sold umbrellas! – and bought the largest umbrella in the shop. How odd!

But Mr Silly knew what he was doing. The big umbrella kept him dry as he wallpapered his house. In different patterns. On the OUTSIDE! How silly!

LITTLE MISS SCATTERBRAIN'S TEA PARTY

Little Miss Scatterbrain is a little bit forgetful. Well, let's be honest, she is VERY forgetful.

She asked some friends to a tea party, and then forgot all about it. When Miss Splendid knocked at the door she said, "Oh, hello, Miss Star, what do you want?"

"Well, really!" said Miss Splendid.

"You've forgotten, haven't you?" asked another guest, Miss Lucky.

"Forgotten what?" Miss Scatterbrain replied.

Miss Scatterbrain took her guests' hats and put them in a cupboard. But at the end of the tea party she couldn't remember which hat belonged to which guest!

Can you help her? Match the right hat to each guest.

Miss Splendid

Miss Dotty

Miss Lucky

Miss Fickle

Miss Neat

1

2

3

4

5

33

LITTLE MISS CURIOUS'S
TRUE OR FALSE QUIZ

Little Miss Curious wants to know about anything and everything. Do you know what her favourite words are? They are WHY? and WHEN? and WHO? and WHERE? and HOW?

"Why not try my quiz? It's all about my little Miss friends. Just answer TRUE or FALSE to each question. Good luck!"

1. Miss Fickle lives in Dandelion Cottage, Sunnytown. True or false?

2. Miss Fun has a pink ribbon in her hair. True or false?

3. The wizard who put magic boots on Miss Bossy's feet is called William. True or false?

MUDDLE TOWN

4. Miss Contrary lives in Muddleland. True or false?

5. Miss Somersault is pink. True or false?

6. Earlybird Cottage is where Miss Late lives. True or false?

7. Miss Tiny lives in a mousehole in the dining room of Home Farm. True or false?

8. Miss Busy wears a pair of big blue glasses. True or false?

9. Miss Shy wears a big red hat. True or false?

10. Miss Dotty lives in Sillyland. True or false?

Answers:
1. True, 2. False – it is blue,
3. False – his name is Wilfred,
4. True, 5. False – she is blue,
6. True, 7. True, 8. False –
they are red, 9. False – she
doesn't wear a hat at all!,
10. False – she lives in
Nonsenseland.

34

MR. NONSENSE'S PUZZLE

"Hello, Mr Nonsense here. I'm just dashing off for a porridge sandwich with my friend, sensible Mr Silly, but before I go I've got a little puzzle for you. Mr Silly painted these two pictures of me. They look the same, but there are five things that are different in the bottom picture. Can you tell me what they are?"

Answers:
1. Mr Nonsense's hat is blue, 2. One of his gloves is missing, 3. His nose is smaller, 4. His shoes have no soles, 5. The grass has changed colour from blue to green.

35

MR. MESSY
MEETS
MR NEAT
AND
MR TIDY

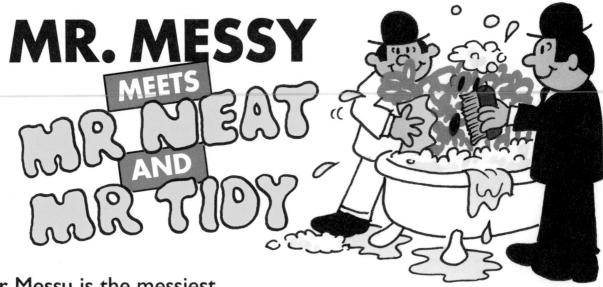

Mr Messy is the messiest
person you could ever imagine.
    One day Mr Neat and Mr Tidy came to Mr Messy's house.
They were going to make Mr Messy look neat and tidy.
What a job!
    Mr Neat washed Mr Messy. Mr Tidy scrubbed him.
    Soon Mr Messy didn't look messy any more.
    "There! Don't you feel better now that you're tidy?"
asked Mr Neat.
     "And neat?" asked Mr Tidy.
    Mr Messy didn't say anything. He just looked miserable.
    Mr Messy went for a walk. He met Mr Sneeze.
    "Hello," said Mr Sneeze. "Why are you
looking so sad?"
    Mr Messy opened his mouth, but before he could say a word,
Mr Sneeze sneezed. He sneezed a very, very BIG
sneeze. ATISHOO!
    The sneeze blew Mr Messy to the ground and rolled him
              around. Bits of soil and grass stuck to him. The
              sneeze blew Mr Messy into a big bush.
              Bits of twigs and leaves stuck to him.
              Now Mr Messy didn't look neat
              and tidy any more. He was messy.
              Very messy. But he didn't mind.
              He felt happy again!
                   Mr Messy was just as he liked
              to be – MESSY!

ATISHOO

NAUGHTY
LITTLE
MISS NAUGHTY

Little Miss Naughty likes being naughty. She is naughty all the time.

One day Miss Quick was doing a jigsaw puzzle. Naughty Miss Naughty mixed up the last two pieces with three pieces from another puzzle. Naughty girl!

Can you find the two pieces that finish the jigsaw puzzle as quickly as Miss Quick can?

1

2

3

4

5

Answer:
Pieces 2 and 5 will finish the jigsaw puzzle.

MR. SMALL AND THE JELLYBEANS

Oh dear! Mr Small has fallen into a big jar of jellybeans.
They are as small as he is! Can you find him?

LITTLE MISS TINY'S
PUZZLE

Little Miss Tiny is very, very small. Tiny, in fact. She lives in a mousehole in the dining room of Home Farm. Here are two pictures of Miss Tiny in her home. Can you find three things that are different in the second picture? Look carefully – the differences are very, very ... tiny!

Answers:

1. Part of Miss Tiny's hair bow is missing, 2. In the picture on the wall the door is green instead of yellow, 3. Part of the pattern on the arm of Miss Tiny's armchair is missing.

MR. BUMP
AND THE TYRES

1. Mr Bump just could not help having little accidents. If there was something to bump into, he was sure to bump into it!

2. Mr Bump was walking along the street. He didn't see the lamp-post and bumped into it, BUMP! Poor Mr Bump!

3. Mr Bump sat down, BUMP!, and rubbed his nose. "By dose does feel very dore," he sighed, rubbing it.

4. Mr Bump walked into the park. He didn't see the stone steps in front of him. He tripped and fell, rolling over and over.

5. Mr Bump landed at the bottom of the steps and sat down, BUMP! His head was very sore. Very sore indeed. Poor Mr Bump!

6. Mr Bump slipped on a banana skin that some careless person had left lying on the ground. Up into the air he went.

7. Mr Bump landed on the ground, BUMP! He picked himself up and rubbed his sore bottom. He was fed up of this.

8. Mr Bump saw a shop selling car tyres. He smiled. Those tyres gave him an idea. A very good idea. He went inside.

9. Mr Bump bought three soft, fat tyres from the shop. He put them on. "Now I won't bump myself when I bump!" he said.

MR. SNOW'S
PROBLEM

"Please help me, you see my hat and my nose and my scarf have blown off and they have got all mixed up with the other hats and noses and scarves, and I need help to find the ones I should be wearing."

Phew! Mr Snow is a talkative sort of snowman, isn't he?
Can you find the hat, nose and scarf he should be wearing?

Answer:
Scarf 1, hat 3 and nose 1

MR. FUSSY
GOES FOR A DRIVE

Mr Fussy likes things to be just so. He is VERY fussy.

Mr Fussy likes to keep his car spick and span. He always cleans and polishes it before he goes out for a drive. And when he gets back!

One morning Mr Fussy polished his car until it shone, then drove off.

Suddenly he stopped. It had started to rain. Plip, plop!

As quickly as he could, Mr Fussy drove his car back into the garage. He didn't want it to get wet!

A few minutes later Mr Fussy looked outside. "Hurray! The rain has stopped!" he said, and he drove his car out of the garage again.

But this time the wind was blowing hard. Leaves and dust blew around. "I'm going back home before my car is covered in dust!" said Mr Fussy.

Mr Fussy drove back into his garage and cleaned and polished his car all over again. You are fussy, Mr Fussy!

Mr Fussy was soon busy with wood and tools inside his garage. He was building something. What could it be? Can you guess?

The next time Mr Fussy went for a drive, he took his garage with him. Now his car never gets wet or dirty! Clever Mr Fussy!

44

All About
MR. CLUMSY

colour:	green
nose:	yellow
shoes:	with untied laces
hair:	untidy
moustache:	scruffy
home:	a scruffy house in the middle of a field
favourite word:	whoops!
title:	Clumsiest Person in the World

45

THE MR. MEN AND LITTLE MISS RUNNING RACE

Mr Rush is the fastest thing on two feet. This year he and little Miss Quick have helped their friends train for a special team running race. Which team will win, the Mr Men or the little Misses?

Play this game with a friend to find out who wins. You need a die and six counters each.

Choose which of you will play for the Mr Men team, and which will play for the little Misses team.

Take it in turns to shake a die. If you shake the number 1, put a counter on top of the Mr Man or little Miss wearing that number.

When you shake a 2, put a counter on the runner wearing a number 2, and so on.

The winner is the first one who covers all 6 runners in his or her team.

A LESSON FOR MR. MEAN

1. Mr Mean is a real meanie. He has lots of money, but he doesn't like spending it. To teach him a lesson a magician put a spell on him.

2. Now, when Mr Mean is mean, funny things happen to him. When he refused to buy a charity flag, his ears turned into apples.

3. Mr Mean's nose turned into a big red strawberry and his fingers into bananas. His feet turned into big green melons.

4. Mr Mean looked like a fruit shop on legs. Hungry Mr Greedy chased him down the road. That will teach you a lesson, Mr Mean!

MR. JELLY'S UPSIDE-DOWN FRUITY Jelly

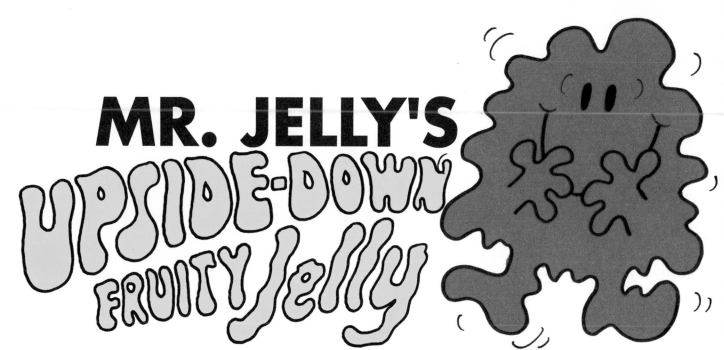

Mr Jelly likes to eat – jelly! He likes jelly with fruit in it best of all. Why not try making some? Remember that kitchens can be dangerous places. NEVER MAKE THINGS IN THE KITCHEN WITHOUT A GROWN-UP TO HELP YOU.

YOU WILL NEED:
150g packet strawberry jelly
150g packet lime jelly
225g tin peach slices
425g tin mandarin oranges
6 glacé cherries

1. Ask a grown-up to help you mix the strawberry jelly with water. Follow the instructions on the packet.
2. Drain the juice from the peaches.
3. Put the cherries and peaches into a 1-litre glass dish. Make a pattern.
4. Pour the strawberry jelly over the fruit. Leave to set.
5. Make the lime jelly. Leave to cool slightly.
6. Drain the oranges. Put them on top of the strawberry jelly, making a pattern.
7. Pour the lime jelly over the oranges. Leave to set.
8. Ask a grown-up to dip the base of the bowl in hot water for a few seconds. Put a plate on top of the bowl. Hold the bowl and plate together, turn upside-down and give them a sharp shake. The dish should lift off the upside-down fruity jelly.

Try eating my jelly with yogurt.
Delicious!

MR. WRONG
AND THE HATS

Whatever Mr Wrong does is absolutely, totally, completely, utterly wrong. He just can't do anything right. He was using a special machine to suck up all the leaves in the garden, but he pressed the wrong button and the machine blew instead of sucked. WHOOSH! Oh, dear! Mr Wrong blew the hats off six Mr Men, as well as his own!

Can you help Mr Wrong give the RIGHT hats back to the Mr Men? Match the numbered hats to their owners.

Mr Slow

Mr Grumble

Mr Wrong

Mr Brave

Mr Grumpy

1

2

3

4

Mr Lazy

5

6

7

Mr Cheerful

50

LITTLE MISS TIDY
AND THE SHOES

Little Miss Tidy likes things to be just so.
She likes putting things in their proper places.
The problem is that she sometimes forgets where she has tidied things away to!

One day Miss Tidy was helping out in the shoe shop. When the customers took off their own shoes so that they could try on lots of new ones, Miss Tidy soon tidied their shoes away. She put them into a big box. But, oh dear, when the customers were ready to leave, their shoes were all mixed up!

Can you help little Miss Tidy to match the right shoes to their owners?

Miss Stubborn   Miss Chatterbox   Miss Helpful   Miss Magic   Miss Quick

Answers:
1 Miss Magic, 2 Miss Helpful,
3 Miss Stubborn, 4 Miss Quick,
5 Miss Chatterbox

52

MR. PERFECT'S WORD PUZZLE

Mr Perfect is perfect in every way.
One day he wrote the names of some Mr Men.
Neatly. Each letter on a square of paper.

"Perfect, aren't they?" Mr Perfect said to Mr Mischief.

Mr Mischief was very naughty. He picked up the pieces of paper and threw them up into the air. They were all mixed up. "Oh, mischief, glorious mischief!" he cried.

Mr Muddle came along. "Please help me sort out this mess!" said Mr Perfect.

Mr Muddle tried, but he couldn't get anything right. The letters were still muddled.

Can you help? Try to find the names of 8 Mr Men in the word square. Look across and down the grid, and forwards and backwards.

Look for these Mr Men:	
BRAVE	DAYDREAM
DIZZY	MISCHIEF
MUDDLE	SKINNY
TALL	WORRY

D	A	Y	D	R	E	A	M
A	B	N	I	C	P	M	I
G	F	N	Z	L	Y	N	S
B	E	I	Z	O	R	Q	C
R	T	K	Y	D	R	R	H
A	A	S	T	S	O	I	I
V	L	W	U	H	W	J	E
E	L	D	D	U	M	K	F

53

LITTLE MISS BOSSY
AND THE BOSSY BOOTS

Some words are missing from this story. Can you decide what they are? The little picture clues will help you.

Little Miss Bossy went for a walk. She met

"Where are you going?" he asked.

"Mind your own business!" said little Miss Bossy.

She met   , who was singing. "Shut up!" she told him. Bossily.

She met   . "Take that silly   off your face!" she said.

Wilfred the wizard decided to do something about little Miss Bossy. He opened a big red   and read the page called HOW TO STOP PEOPLE BEING BOSSY.

The next day Miss Bossy met   . He was fast asleep. "Wake up!" she cried.

Wilfred the wizard was watching. He said a special wizardy word and, as if by magic, a pair of   were on little Miss Bossy's   .

The magic boots marched little Miss Bossy along. *Left, right, left, right.* Faster and faster. She couldn't do a thing about it. *Left, right, left, right.* Then they stopped.

Miss Bossy tried to take the boots off. It was impossible.

Along came . "Those boots are for people who are too bossy," he told her.

"Take them off AT ONCE!" shouted little Miss Bossy. "DO AS I SAY!"

The magic boots set off again. *Left, right, left, right.* For miles and miles.

When they stopped along came Wilfred. "MAKE THESE GO AWAY!" shouted Miss Bossy. Very bossily.

"Only if you say the magic word," said Wilfred.

Miss Bossy thought. And thought. And thought again. "Please," she said.

The boots disappeared!

"Now stop being bossy," said Wilfred, wagging his "or you know what will happen."

From then on little Miss Bossy was a changed person. Not bossy at all. You know why, don't you? Yes, she is afraid of those bossy boots!

All About Little Miss Bossy

colour:	blue
hat:	red, with a yellow band and a white flower
likes:	being bossy
dislikes:	those bossy boots!

55

MR. IMPOSSIBLE Goes Flying

Mr Impossible flapped his arms
And found that he could fly!
So he flapped and flapped, and flapped and flew
Right up into the sky!

He landed on the moon with ease!
And guess what he did find?
He found the moon was made of cheese
And he'd landed on the rind!

LITTLE MISS BUSY'S BUSY DAY

Little Miss Busy is busy from morning till night. She gets up at three o'clock in the morning, before it is even light, and doesn't go to bed until midnight. Busy, busy, busy, that's her!

Little Miss Busy has an extra job today – she's helping to deliver some parcels for the postman. But little Miss Naughty has written out new labels for the parcels. She has jumbled up the letters of the names of the little Misses the parcels are for.

Can you rearrange the letters to help Miss Busy deliver the right parcel to the right little Miss?

1. MISS SEIW

2. MISS BOULTRE

3. MISS HNISUSEN

4. MISS TALE

5. MISS NUF

Answers:
The little Misses are
1. Wise, 2. Trouble,
3. Sunshine, 4. Late,
5. Fun.

57

YOU COULD WIN A CRACKING TOWNSEND BIKE

IF YOU KNOW WHICH MR MAN EATS LOTS OF EGGS!

Hey Mister - or Miss!
How would you like to win one of these exciting, new kids' bikes from Townsend. In all the latest colours - and packed with features - Townsend Bikes really are the business for kids on the block! Enter now, it's easy.

PEANUT
FINISHED IN JUNGLE RED, THIS BOY'S 12" WHEEL ATB-STYLE BIKE FEATURES HI-RISE HANDLEBARS, MAG WHEELS, TRAINING WHEELS, PNEUMATIC BLACK TYRES, PADDED SADDLE, FULL BALLBEARING ONE PIECE CRANK AND FULLY ENCLOSED CHAINGUARD.

DRAGON
FINISHED IN DRAGON BREATH RED, THIS BOY'S 14" WHEEL ATB-STYLE BIKE FEATURES HI-RISE HANDLEBARS, MAG WHEELS, TRAINING WHEELS, CHUNKY TYRES, PADDED SADDLE, OVERSIZE DOWNTUBE, FULL BALLBEARING ONE PIECE CRANK AND FULLY ENCLOSED CHAINGUARD.

PIXIE
FINISHED IN NEON PINK & WHITE, THIS GIRL'S 12" WHEEL ATB-STYLE BIKE FEATURES HI-RISE HANDLEBARS, MAG WHEELS, TRAINING WHEELS, DOLL CARRIER, PNEUMATIC WHITE TYRES, PADDED SADDLE, FULL BALLBEARING ONE PIECE CRANK AND FULLY ENCLOSED CHAINGUARD.

Prizes are courtesy of Townsend Cycles

TOWNSEND
TOWNSEND CYCLES LTD. HORIZON PARK, GREEN FOLD WAY. HOPE CARR, LEIGH, LANCASHIRE WN7 3XH.

HOW TO ENTER

It's easy! All you have to do is answer this simple question:

Which Mr Man eats lots of eggs?

Write the answer on a postcard or envelope, with your name, age and address (together with your preference for type of bicycle).
Send to:
Mr. Men Annual 1996 Competition, Marketing Department, Egmont Publishing, PO Box III, Great Ducie Street, Manchester M60 3BL.

Closing date: Ist February 1996.

The first correct entry selected at random after the closing date will win a super new Townsend bicycle of their choice. The next 100 selected will win a runner-up prize.

PLUS 100 RUNNERS-UP PRIZES

20 MR. MEN DOT TO DOT BOOKS
40 MR. MEN STORY STICKER BOOKS
40 MR. MEN AUDIO CASSETTES

Courtesy of World International and Cassettes for Young People.

RULES
Employees of World International or their respective agents may not enter this competition. The Editor's decision is final and no correspondence will be entered into. A list of winners' names will be available on request and on receipt of a SAE after 14th February 1996. The Publishers reserve the right to vary the prizes, subject to availability at the time of judging the competition.

58

COMPETITION

MR. CHATTERBOX
ON THE TELEPHONE

Mr Chatterbox is one of those people who just cannot stop talking. He talks to anybody and everybody about anything and everything.

Can you find out who he is talking to today? Follow the tangle of telephone wires to find out.

Little Miss Giggles

Mr Muddle

Mr Dizzy

Little Miss Chatterbox

59

Mr Brave

Mr Noisy

LITTLE MISS BRAINY'S QUIZ

Little Miss Brainy knows everything, or at least she THINKS she does! See if you know as much as (or more than!) Miss Brainy does about her Mr Men and little Miss friends by trying this quiz. You will finds lots of the answers in this annual!

1. Which timid little Miss lives in Thimble Cottage?

2. What is Mr Strong's favourite food?

3. Which Mr Man lives in a teapot?

4. Which little Miss wants to be famous?

5. What colour is Mr Small's hat?

6. Which little Miss lives in Chuckle Cottage?

7. Which two Mr Men wear glasses?

8. What colour are the little Miss Twins?

9. Which Mr Man wears a red and white striped scarf around his neck?

10. Which little Miss loves to eat sausages?

60

Answers:
1. Miss Shy, 2. Eggs, 3. Mr Funny, 4. Miss Star, 5. Blue, 6. Miss Giggles, 7. Mr Clever and Mr Brave (Mr Uppity wears a monocle on one eye!), 8. Yellow, 9. Mr Snow, 10. Miss Greedy.

MR. UPPITY SAVES THE DAY

1. Mr Greedy sent party invitations to all his Mr Men friends. Mr Uppity drove by in his big car. "See you at the party, old chap!" said Mr Uppity.

2. On the day of the party Mr Greedy got lots of food ready. "I'll taste a cake, just one," he said.

3. When the Mr Men arrived the table was empty. "Where's the food?" asked Mr Uppity. "In here," said Mr Greedy, pointing to his big fat tum. Greedy Mr Greedy had eaten the party food. All of it!

4. Mr Uppity took the Mr Men outside. His big car was full of food. "I've been to one of Mr Greedy's no-food parties before," he said. "Tuck in everyone." Good old Mr Uppity!